# ABOUT

# *MARTIN LUTHER KING DAY*

## *MARY VIRGINIA FOX*

**ENSLOW PUBLISHERS, INC.**

Bloy St. & Ramsey Ave.,     P.O. Box 38
Box 777                     Aldershot
Hillside, N.J. 07205     Hants GU12 6BP
U.S.A.                      U.K.

**Library of Congress Cataloging-in-Publication Data**

Fox, Mary Virginia
    About Martin Luther King Day / by Mary Virginia Fox.
        p. cm.
    Bibliography: p.
    Includes index.
    Summary: Presents the history of the holiday named for civil rights leader Martin Luther
King, Jr., celebrated on the third Monday of every January.
    ISBN 0-89490-200-8
    1. Martin Luther King Day—Juvenile literature. 2. King, Martin Luther, Jr., 1929-1968—
Anniversaries, etc.—Juvenile literature. 3. King, Martin Luther, Jr., 1929- 1968—Juvenile
literature. 4. Afro- Americans—Biography—Juvenile literature. 5. Afro- Americans—Civil
rights—Juvenile literature. 6. Baptists—United States—Clergy—Biography—Juvenile literature. [1. Martin Luther King Day. 2. King, Martin Luther, Jr., 1929-1968.] I. Title.
E185.97.K5F68   1989
394.2'68—dc19       88-23230
                CIP
                AC

Printed in the United States of America

10 9 8 7 6 5 4 3 2 1

**Illustration Credits:**
AP/Wide World Photos, pp. 4, 33, 37; © 1988 Robert Sengstacke, pp. 52, 57, 58; Estate of
Martin Luther King, Jr., p. 4; John Fitzgerald Kennedy Library, p. 41; Moorland-Springarn
Research Center, pp. 21, 23; Pete Souza/White House, p. 8; Schomburg Center for Research
in Black Culture/The New York Public Library/Astor, Lenox and Tilden Foundation, pp. 11,
14, 17, 20, 25, 26, 27, 29, 42, 47, 54; Washington, D.C. Public Schools, p. 55 and cover.

# Contents

Martin Luther King, Jr. 1929–1968

# 1

## *Making It a Holiday*

On the third Monday in January, schools are closed. Postal workers and bankers get the day off. Every federal office in the country shuts down. It is a day for parades, speeches, and prayers. On this day, we honor Martin Luther King, Jr. We remember the changes that he brought about in this country and around the world.

It took an act of Congress to make this day a national holiday. More than fifteen years went by from the death of Martin Luther King, Jr. before the legislation was passed.

First, a bill had to be introduced by a member of the House of Representatives. The Speaker of the House then assigned the bill to a committee, whose members discussed the matter in detail. Meetings were held where people with opposing ideas could state their positions. The committee finally reported that they felt the bill should be put to a vote, but still another group of legislators, the Rules Committee, had to schedule the debate on the issue.

When the House of Representatives passed the bill by a vote of 338 to 90, it was sent to the Senate. Here again, the issue had to pass through committee discussion and public hearings before a final vote was taken.

The final barrier to honoring King fell on October 4, 1983 when Senator Jesse Helms, from the state of North Carolina, gave up his one-man fight to defeat the bill. Helms had denounced King as a communist.

Helms outraged many in the Congress. Senator Edward Kennedy accused him of "red smear" tactics. Representative William Gray termed his words "shoddy and sordid." Even Senator Strom Thurmond, who had been against civil rights bills in the 1950s and 1960s, urged Helms to stop his "mean and unjust" fight.

Why was anyone against having the holiday? Some people pointed out that only two other individuals, George Washington and Christopher Columbus, were honored by national holidays. Why hadn't Abraham Lincoln, Franklin Delano Roosevelt, Dwight Eisenhower, or John F. Kennedy, all great Americans, been given such an honor?

Other critics said if we were trying to make up for the way we treated blacks during slavery, we should honor an Indian hero too. These people had also suffered prejudice. King's admirers pointed out that King's greatness was being recognized because he had been able to bring about social change through peaceful means, not by war or revolution.

Those who still opposed the idea claimed that we had enough holidays. This would make the tenth. The Congressional Budget Office estimated it would cost $18 million for extra overtime pay to federal employees who had to work on a federal holiday and another $220 million to pay employees for a day on which they were not working.

Senator Robert Dole countered with, "I suggest they hurry back to their pocket calculators and estimate the cost of 300 years of slavery, followed by a century or more of economic, political and social exclusion and discrimination."

In every session of Congress following Dr. King's assassination, members had introduced legislation calling for the holiday. Even before the holiday was official, countless blacks took it upon themselves to stay home from school or work on January 15. Thousands wrote letters and signed petitions voicing support of the observance. On January 15, 1981, one hundred thousand marchers met in Washington, D.C., to show their support for the holiday.

The bill was finally passed by both the House of Representatives and the Senate and was signed into law by President Reagan on November 2, 1983. This happened 366 years after the first black slaves landed on the shores of the New World at Jamestown, Virginia; 122 years after the signing of the Emancipation Proclamation freeing the slaves after the Civil War; and 31 years after the Supreme Court declared that all kinds of segregation between whites and blacks were illegal. The first national celebration of the King holiday did not take place until January 20, 1986, so the states had a chance to change their laws. However, a few states had already declared King's birthday a state holiday without waiting for congressional action.

In 1987, Arizona's Governor Evan Mecham canceled the holiday honoring Martin Luther King, Jr., saying that it would be necessary to put the issue before a vote within the state. "Let the court of last resort—the people—decide," he said.

The nation had already decided. To know why we should celebrate this holiday, we should remember the injustices that King was trying to fight. He fought for freedom, equality, and dignity for all races, and he accomplished this through nonviolent means. He tried to better the lives of the poor. He was a leader for world peace.

President Reagan urged each state to decide on a tribute to King. He spoke to students from the White House, saying, "Ours is a better country today. Each of you has more potential, more opportunity, because of the hard work and courage of one remarkable individual."

President Reagan signing the bill creating the holiday honoring Martin Luther King, Jr.

# 2

# *Beginning of Slavery*

The first blacks came to the New World, not in chains, but as explorers and servants. One of Columbus's crew was a black man named Pedro Alonso Niño. Thirty African Negroes were with Balboa in 1513 when he discovered the Pacific Ocean. When Spanish and Portuguese explorers came to North America, blacks were with them. Blacks accompanied the Jesuit missionaries who claimed the Mississippi River Valley for France.

When the first group of white settlers came to this country from Europe, they brought white, indentured servants with them. In return for the opportunity to come to this country, these men and women had voluntarily agreed to work without wages for a certain number of years, usually seven. At the end of that time they had earned their freedom and a chance to start a new life. Often they became successful, respected citizens.

As the first settlements began to prosper and the forests were cleared for farming, there was a need for strong men and women to work the fields. Twenty slaves were brought to Jamestown, Virginia, in 1619, but it was not until the end of the century that great numbers of slaves were imported from Africa to work on large plantations.

The demand for labor became greater than the supply of indentured servants. European traders made deals with African chieftains to enslave their neighbors. Human lives were sold for very little. Men, women, and children were kidnapped and driven like cattle to seaports where Dutch, Portuguese, and English ships waited.

They were packed below decks into inhumanly crowded quarters. There was hardly room to sit or lie down. They were chained together to make escape impossible. There was little food or fresh water. There were no toilets. The suffering was terrible.

Disease cut the number of slaves ready for the auction block, and those who did survive had little to look forward to. There was never a guarantee that families would be sold together. Some plantation owners tried to show mercy, but they didn't think it unfair to expect slaves to work twelve hours a day, seven days a week.

For the next 150 years the agricultural work force, particularly in the South, was made up of black slaves. The staple cash crops for export were cotton, tobacco, rice, and sugar. From planting to harvest, hard hours of labor were needed. Farming in the northern colonies was usually on a smaller scale, but slaves were used as household help and for building and for mining iron and coal. They were always given the hardest, meanest jobs.

Few Europeans knew anything about the huge continent of Africa with its many nations. They were unaware of the rich cultural heritage of these people. These slaves had black skin. They looked different. Most slave owners did not consider blacks to be their equal in intelligence. They therefore also assumed their emotional capacity must be limited and their suffering unimportant. Yet time and again blacks proved they could act with bravery and brilliance.

One such person was Crispus Attucks, a runaway slave who worked on ships sailing out of Boston Harbor. He led a group of fellow sailors in an attack against a post of British soldiers during the American Revolution. The soldiers fired on the unarmed crew. This event was

An example of one of the houses where blacks lived during slavery

known as the Boston Massacre, and Attucks was the first to be killed.

His bravery was praised by everyone. It surprised many colonists that someone who had so little freedom in his own life was ready to fight for it.

At first blacks were barred from enlisting on the side of the colonists in the Revolutionary War. But when they joined the British army with a promise of freedom, the rules were changed, and blacks were allowed in the American army.

When it came time to write a constitution for the new country, no mention of outlawing slavery was included. Some of our early statesmen opposed the idea of slavery, but cooperation among the representatives of the thirteen colonies was very precarious. A fight on this issue might have ended the process of writing the Constitution. Therefore, the rights of blacks and women were ignored.

Representation in Congress was determined according to the population of each state, but a slave was not even counted as a whole person. When the government figured on the number of people living in a southern state, it recorded a slave as three-fifths of a person. A planter who owned ten slaves had, in effect, six votes, while a citizen in a free state had one vote. The South had won a victory.

On March 2, 1807, President Thomas Jefferson signed into law a bill that made it illegal to bring new slaves into the country, but the law was poorly enforced. At this time there were over one million blacks already in the United States.

Even without new slaves from Africa, the black population continued to increase. Slave owners were delighted when black children were born to parents they owned. Each baby was worth at least $200 on the slave market.

Only in a few instances were black men and women given an education to improve their conditions. When opportunities were provided, they proved to have equal intelligence to whites.

A good example was Benjamin Banneker. Born in 1731, he attended a Quaker-run private school open to whites and blacks in Baltimore, Maryland. He showed a special interest in mathematics and science. This brought him to the attention of a Quaker, George Ellicott, who further helped Banneker by lending him books on mathematics and astronomy. Going to school helped Banneker develop his mathematical ability. Soon he was able to publish his own almanac, accurately predicting solar eclipses and other astronomical data.

He sent a copy to Thomas Jefferson with a letter asking for more liberal laws for blacks. Jefferson praised him, but nothing was done to help other blacks. Yet Banneker was honored by being appointed to a commission to draw the boundary line and lay out the streets of the District of Columbia, the new national capital.

Massachusetts was the most liberal state toward blacks. A law was passed allowing free Afro-Americans who paid taxes all the privileges of citizenship and a voice in local government.

In 1780 Paul Cuffe, a black man, began to build ships. His business prospered. After joining the Quaker religious faith, he set about trying to improve conditions for blacks. He gathered together thirty-eight blacks who wanted to return to Africa and paid for their transportation with his own money. This was hardly the answer to the nation's problems, but it showed others the concern and resourcefulness of one black man.

Blacks were learning to improve their own living conditions. The Negro Baptists in Georgia and the Bethel African Methodist Episcopal Church in the North were sources of moral support to their members.

Some blacks, like Harriet Tubman, devoted their lives to helping their people. She managed to escape to freedom herself, but she returned many times to lead others to safety.

Harriet Tubman

John Brown took matters even further. He organized a small attack force to seize weapons stored at Harpers Ferry, Virginia. He meant to arm a small band of blacks so they could set other slaves free. The plot failed, and John Brown was hanged.

A number of whites continued to fight against slavery. They were called abolitionists, because they wanted to abolish (put an end to) slavery completely. In 1852 Harriet Beecher Stowe wrote a novel called *Uncle Tom's Cabin* that told of the brutality of slavery. It was said that for every book sold, a hundred whites converted to the side of the abolitionists.

As more territory was added to the western frontier, Congress tried to keep peace by maintaining a balance of free states and slave states. But even when a slave master moved to a free state, his slaves were not considered free.

In 1832 an army surgeon living in St. Louis, Missouri, purchased a black man named Dred Scott as his slave. In later years the slave owner moved to the free territory of Minnesota. It was here that Dred Scott was married, and here that his wife gave birth to their first child.

When Scott's owner died in 1843, Scott tried to buy freedom for himself and his family. It was denied. He then resorted to legal action, claiming that living in a free territory meant he was no longer a slave. The issue was debated in several courts, but finally in 1857 the Supreme Court decided that Dred Scott could not be considered a free man. As a black man he could not claim privileges as a citizen.

It was not long before those laws were to be changed.

# 3

## The End of Slavery

There were many economic reasons why the North and South went to war, but the most obvious reason was the question of slavery. On January 1, 1863, President Lincoln declared that all slaves were to be set free. But where were they to go?

When the Civil War started in the spring of 1861, some black men fought for the South in defense of the land where they had been born, but many others escaped behind enemy lines to join the North. For those who did not join the armies, it was hard to find food and shelter. The big plantations of the South, for the most part, were left untended. The economy of the country suffered.

On April 9, 1865, with the surrender of the Southern army at Appomattox, Virginia, the war was over. There followed a period of Reconstruction, when the country torn apart by civil war tried to heal itself, but peace was long in coming.

On December 18, 1865 the Thirteenth Amendment to the Constitution of the United States was passed abolishing slavery. The Fourteenth Amendment, which became a part of the Constitution on July 28, 1868, established rights of citizenship for former slaves, and the Fifteenth Amendment, ratified March 30, 1870, gave them the right to vote. With the power of the government behind them, all things seemed possible. Yet these dreams soon faded.

The states that had seceded from the Union—Virginia, North and South Carolina, Georgia, Florida, Alabama, Tennessee, Mississippi, Arkansas, Louisiana, and Texas—had to rewrite their constitutions. For a time it seemed blacks would be able to take over local government in the South. The voters of South Carolina elected 87 blacks and 40 whites to the state House of Representatives, although the whites controlled the state Senate and the office of governor. There was fear that blacks would try to get even with their former masters, many of

Black soldiers who fought in the Union Army during the Civil War: the 4th U.S. Colored Infantry at Fort Lincoln

whom could not vote because of their military service during the war.

It was a time of confusion and corruption. There were men from the North who hurried south to pick up whatever profits they could steal. During this time of Reconstruction, bitter anger flared between the races.

Twenty blacks served in the House of Representatives in Washington, but they received little cooperation even from members of their own party. The whites banded together "to put blacks in their place." They did this by setting up state rules that would take the vote away from blacks. They barred everyone who could not read the Constitution from voting. A tax was charged for the privilege of voting. Polling places were changed without notice. Stuffing ballot boxes (adding illegal votes) was a common practice. "We can outcount them," the dishonest bragged.

When all else failed, whites turned to terror tactics. This was the beginning of the Ku Klux Klan, an organization of whites whose aim was to control blacks and drive them from power. There were many terrible tales of beatings and lynchings (illegal hangings). It is no wonder that many blacks gave up their fight.

There were those who felt the one way to secure peace in the South was to keep the races apart. The segregation laws were called "Jim Crow" laws. No one knows for sure where this term came from. It may have been copied from the name of a black comedian who performed a song-and-dance routine in an old-time musical show.

Schools and parks were segregated. Blacks drank from separate water fountains, and they used segregated waiting rooms and lavatories. They received the poorest health care and housing.

A civil rights act of 1875 declared that no one could be turned away from an inn or train or other form of transportation, but time after time, when the law was put to the test in courts, blacks lost their case.

Many blacks moved to the cities in the North to search for higher-paying jobs. They often found terrible living conditions for their families and jobs that barely paid for food on the table. Housing was available only in the poorest and most run-down parts of cities. Even those few who could have afforded somewhat better homes were not allowed to move out of the black ghettos.

Not all black leaders agreed on solutions for the problems facing their race. Booker T. Washington, a well-known educator who headed Tuskegee Institute, a vocational school for blacks, proposed a compromise. He felt that blacks must learn to live as second-class citizens until they could better themselves through education, thrift, and hard work. William Edward Burghardt (W.E.B.) DuBois, a pioneer black scholar, felt his race should be more aggressive in demanding their rights of citizenship.

In May of 1910, the National Association for the Advancement of Colored People (NAACP) was formed. The purpose of the NAACP was to do away with racial prejudice and to fight for complete equality under the law. This was a tall order, but over the years some of their goals have been met.

In 1911, three groups interested in the problems of blacks in New York City joined to form the National

Urban League. Its purpose was to work for better jobs for blacks.

While black leaders were rallying support for their causes, the United States was heading for a world war. In April 1917, a Selective Service Act was passed to draft men into the armed forces. Blacks volunteered in large numbers. There were 367,000 inducted into the army, yet none were taken into the marines and only a few were accepted by the navy, specifically for menial jobs. There were no black pilots. Blacks sought the same opportunities as white soldiers for the privilege of being trained as officers. Only a very small number received these promotions.

Black troops were housed in separate quarters and trained in segregated groups, something they bitterly resented. A. Philip Randolph, who was president of a

A group of influential blacks who in 1909 formed the Niagara Movement, a forerunner of the NAACP

large labor union of sleeping car porters, fought against segregated military training, but it was not until the Korean War in 1953 that the armed forces were completely integrated.

Black combat troops were among the first to be sent overseas in World War I. They were placed in various units of the French army. There they served bravely and were decorated for their gallantry.

The French were far more liberal in their attitude toward blacks than Americans. They treated them as friends and equals, which in some cases made it even harder for the blacks to return to the prejudice in their own country. Most returned home to low-paying jobs and miserable housing conditions in city ghettos.

When the Depression hit in 1929, factories shut down. There was worldwide unemployment. Blacks were the first to suffer. Relief funds were not administered equally. It was a time of desperation for many.

A. Philip Randolph

# 4

# A Leader Is Born

Nineteen twenty-nine is a year to be remembered for many reasons. On January 15, 1929, Martin Luther King, Jr., was born in Atlanta, Georgia. His father was the minister of the Ebenezer Baptist Church, as his grandfather had been before him.

Martin Luther King, Sr., saw the suffering of his people. He worked very hard to break down the barriers between races, urging his congregation to register their complaints by voting in elections. But it was a time when many people were working so hard just to feed their families that they didn't have time for politics.

Young Martin, or M. L. as he was called, soon learned that there was discrimination and pure hatred of blacks. By the time he entered school, he was not allowed to play with white children.

During the years of King's childhood, Franklin Delano Roosevelt served as president of the United States from 1933 to 1945. Roosevelt was elected on the Democratic ticket. Blacks had traditionally voted for the Republican party of Abraham Lincoln and against the southern Democrats. Now many of them rallied to the more liberal platform Roosevelt proposed and became Democrats. Roosevelt appointed several blacks to jobs of influence.

The day M. L.'s father heard about the appointment of Mrs. Mary McLeod Bethune as director of negro affairs for the National Youth Association, he planned a sermon on the subject of pride and self-respect. Many blacks felt it was useless to struggle for equality, but here

Eleanor Roosevelt and Mary McLeod Bethune

was a woman pictured in the papers having lunch with Eleanor Roosevelt, wife of the president of the United States, in the White House.

Yet there was still prejudice. On another occasion, when Mrs. Bethune was awarded a special honor for her service in the field of human welfare, she had to walk up six flights of stairs because she refused to ride up in the freight elevator, which was designated for "colored people."

Another woman who had a great influence on public opinion was not a politician but a fine concert singer. Marian Anderson was scheduled to give a concert in Washington, D.C., but the organization that owned the concert hall, the Daughters of the American Revolution (DAR), refused to allow a black to sing there.

It seemed impossible that someone who had performed all over the world would suddenly not be considered qualified to share her talent in her own country. When newspapers printed the story, the DAR office received hundreds of letters, many from white musicians who canceled their own performances in protest. Martin Luther King, Sr., was one of those who wrote expressing hope that one day such bitterness would be overcome. Soon the First Lady invited Anderson to perform at the Lincoln Memorial, and thousands of people attended.

The unemployment rate of blacks during the Depression years was extremely high. There were not enough jobs to go around. Trade unions frequently kept blacks from joining their ranks to keep jobs for white workers.

The first all-black labor organization was the Brotherhood of Sleeping Car Porters. With train transportation being so important for travelers, porters who serviced these trains were much in demand. These porters formed the Brotherhood of Sleeping Car Porters and elected A. Philip Randolph their first president. Members learned how to negotiate for better working conditions.

In other ways blacks found they could help each other. In Pittsburgh, blacks stopped buying milk from a local dairy until black drivers were hired. It was not until after Pearl Harbor was attacked and World War II was declared in 1941 that the nation's factories went into full production. Even then the best jobs went to whites.

Marian Anderson performing

25

Blacks decided to protest by marching on Washington, D.C. Before the march ever took place, Roosevelt called a conference with black leaders to try to solve the problem. A Fair Employment Practices Committee was set up to investigate complaints against discrimination.

"We get more when we yell than when we plead," said Roy Wilkins, head of the NAACP. In other words, aggressive demands yielded results.

Martin Luther King, Jr., would remember those words. For a time he thought seriously of becoming a lawyer or perhaps following his mother's suggestion of being a doctor of medicine. However, the church had always been such an important part of his life that he finally decided to follow in his father's footsteps and become a minister.

Members of the Brotherhood of Sleeping Car Porters

After finishing his work at Morehouse College, he accepted a scholarship at Crozer Theological Seminary in Chester, Pennsylvania. It was the fall of 1948. He was nineteen. He would be living away from home in a white world for the first time.

While in college, King had been much impressed by an essay written by Henry David Thoreau a hundred years earlier, "Civil Disobedience." Thoreau felt that if enough people would follow their conscience and disobey unjust laws, they could bring about a peaceful revolution and win their argument. King also read about the Indian leader Mahatma Gandhi, who had struggled to free his people from British rule by peaceful revolution. These were ideas King was to live by.

Martin Luther King, Jr., as a young man

While at the seminary King met a young woman, Coretta Scott. They were soon married, and in 1954 Martin Luther King, Jr., accepted the job of pastor of the Dexter Avenue Baptist Church in Montgomery, Alabama. He also received his Ph.D., which meant he would now be addressed as Dr. King—except by his closest friends and family, who continued to call him M. L. or Martin. Life seemed to be falling into a quiet, satisfying pattern, but that pattern was soon to be broken.

On December 1, 1955, Mrs. Rosa Parks was on her way home after working a full day as a seamstress in a Montgomery department store. She boarded a bus, as she always did, and found a seat behind the section reserved for white riders. Black riders had to sit in the back of the bus, as part of the segregation policy of the South.

However as the bus began to fill, a white man was forced to stand. This was against the rules that custom had established over the years. No white person should have to stand while black riders were seated.

The bus driver stopped the bus and told four riders in the row closest to the white section that they would have to move since no blacks could sit in the same row as a white. Three of the black passengers seated with Mrs. Parks obeyed. Mrs. Parks was tired. It didn't seem fair that four blacks would have to stand so one white could be seated. She had paid the full fare.

The bus driver warned her that if she didn't follow orders, she would be arrested. Mrs. Parks did not argue, but she would not move. The bus driver put his threat into action. He stopped at the next corner to summon a policeman. Mrs. Parks was arrested and taken to jail.

Mrs. Parks was not the first black to be arrested for the same "crime," but she was well-known in the black community of Montgomery, and word of what had happened soon spread. She had once been secretary to the president of the local NAACP, Mr. E. D. Nixon. He arranged bail for her release.

She might have paid the fine and the incident would have been forgotten, but others came to her defense. Too many blacks had been treated unfairly. Dr. King felt that some kind of protest was necessary. He called a meeting to be held at the Dexter Avenue Baptist Church.

Rosa Parks

More people came than could be seated. They stood in the aisles waiting to hear his words. King told them that the only way they could fight back was to boycott (refuse to use) the buses. Blacks were asked to substitute tired feet for tired souls.

Within twenty-four hours after Mrs. Parks was arrested, pamphlets were printed and distributed throughout the community. No one knew just how well the plan would succeed, but on the morning of December 5 only eight black riders were seen using the bus.

The few blacks who had cars arranged to pick up friends and strangers to take them to work. Most had to walk. Some rode mules. The boycott was a success.

King felt that now was the time to organize for future action. Leaders of the black community called another meeting. They named their organization the Montgomery Improvement Association, and King was elected its president.

The white community fought back with terrorism and harassment by the police. Car-pool drivers were arrested for picking up hitchhikers, which was against the law. Those waiting on street corners for rides were arrested for loitering.

Every day King received hate mail, and on January 30, 1956, his house was bombed while he was in church speaking to a group, urging them to follow the path of nonviolent protest. King rushed home and found his wife and baby daughter safe, but an angry mob of blacks gathered. King spoke to them from his blackened and splintered front porch. He told the crowd to go home and follow the teachings of Jesus.

"We must learn to meet hate with love."

But the attorney for the bus company said, "If we granted the Negroes these demands, they would go about boasting of a victory that they had won over the white people, and this we will not stand for."

Even during the worst of the winter, blacks still turned their backs on the buses. Some were forced to walk many miles to work. It took the United States Supreme Court to end the boycott.

On November 13, 1956, the Court declared Alabama's state and local laws requiring segregation on buses illegal. On December 20, 1956, federal injunctions were served on city and bus company officials forcing them to follow the Supreme Court's decision.

The following day Dr. King and a white minister, Rev. Glen Smiley, shared the front seat of a public bus. They had won their fight. The boycott had lasted 381 days. It had united the community.

Until then, black people had forgotten how to believe in themselves. Martin Luther King, Jr., had helped change that. At age twenty-eight, he received a special medal from the NAACP as the person making the greatest contribution to race relations that year.

# 5

## Freedom Fighter

King had proved that peaceful mass action could bring about change, but there was a lot more work to be done. In January 1957, the Southern Christian Leadership Conference (SCLC) was formed. King was asked to be president. His first action was to ask President Eisenhower for a White House conference on equal rights. The request was denied.

King would not give up. He conferred with two other black leaders: A. Philip Randolph of the Brotherhood of Sleeping Car Porters, the largest black union, and Roy Wilkins, national president of the NAACP. They discussed ways to let the public know how important it was to fight for civil rights legislation.

A mass march on the nation's capital was planned. On May 17, 1957, approximately thirty-seven thousand people gathered in front of the Lincoln Memorial. Many speakers addressed the crowd, but the voice of Martin Luther King, Jr., was the one they had come to hear. He had become the undisputed leader of the civil rights movement.

"Give us the ballot," he said. "We will no longer plead . . . We will write the proper laws . . . We will fill the legislature with men of good will . . . We will get the proper judges who love mercy."

Congress could scarcely ignore the enthusiasm these words inspired. On September 9, 1957, Congress created the Civil Rights Commission and the Civil Rights Division of the Department of Justice. At least there would

Martin Luther King, Jr., addressing a large crowd in Washington, D.C.

be an official body to turn to with the authority to investigate voting irregularities.

The SCLC organized the Crusade for Citizenship in an effort to register five million southern black voters, but whites put every obstacle in their way. They made blacks wait long hours in line during working days to fill out complicated forms. They frequently changed voting districts to lessen the power of the black vote. It was discouraging, but King continued to speak to groups, keeping their hopes alive.

Through his example, he inspired others to take up the fight against injustices. One such person was Daisy Bates. She and her husband published a newspaper in Little Rock, Arkansas, called the *State Press*.

Back in 1954, the Supreme Court had ordered desegregation of public schools, but such a law had not been put into practice in Arkansas. Mrs. Bates was hopeful that with the election of a new governor, Orval Faubus, the process of integration would come about as promised. She urged blacks to test the law.

In 1957, sixty black students asked to be transferred to all-white Central High. Many parents of these students were threatened with loss of their jobs. Students themselves were threatened with beatings if they tried to come to Central.

Nine students were finally accepted as a token number for enrollment. Would they be safe? Mrs. Bates could not answer that question. Her own windows had been broken. Fiery crosses had been burned on her front yard.

On September 5, 1957, when the group of black students arrived at Central High, they were turned away by the state's National Guard under orders of Governor Faubus. President Eisenhower countered by placing the Arkansas National Guard under the authority of the federal government with orders to ensure the rights of the nine black students wanting to attend school.

The next year when the federal troops were recalled, the governor declared that, to ensure order in the community, the schools of Little Rock would remain closed for both blacks and whites. Most white students enrolled in private schools, which left black children with no education at all, except for volunteer at-home teachers.

It took one year of legal action before the schools were opened again. Another victory was won by a group of brave blacks, who refused to fight violence and hatred with force and anger.

King was called constantly to speak to groups all over the country to spread his message to as many people as possible. In order to have time to spend with his family at home, he started to put his words on paper. His first book, *Stride Toward Freedom,* was a great success but almost cost him his life.

He was signing copies of his book in a Harlem, New York, department store when a black woman stepped forward and plunged a letter opener into his chest. She was taken away and later was judged insane. King recovered from his wound, but it took several months before he was strong enough to continue his busy schedule.

In February 1959, he and Coretta accepted an invitation to visit India. "To other countries I go as a tourist," he said, "but to India I come as a pilgrim." India was the homeland of Mahatma Gandhi, whose example of non-violence had greatly influenced King's own philosophy.

When he returned home he made the decision to move to Atlanta, Georgia, where he would be sharing his ministerial duties with his father, pastor of the Ebenezer Baptist Church. King was disappointed that civil rights legislation was progressing so slowly. "The President has proposed a ten-year plan to put a man on the moon," King said. "We do not yet have a plan to put a Negro in the state government of Alabama."

Many were sharing his discontent. Blacks were still not allowed in public areas with whites. On February 1, 1960, four black students sat down at a lunch counter in Greensboro, North Carolina, and refused to move until they were served or arrested. Suddenly these sit-ins, as they were called, began to be organized for any place that segregated blacks. This was the beginning of the Student Nonviolent Coordinating Committee (SNCC).

In October 1960, King and fifty-one other persons were arrested during a sit-in at Rich's department store in Atlanta. The charges were dropped against all the others, but King was sentenced to four months' hard labor in prison. It was claimed that he had been on parole for not having a current Georgia driver's license, and for any second offense, no matter how unimportant, he could be sent to jail.

When the news hit the papers, help came from Senator John Kennedy, who promised that if he were elected president of the country he would do everything in his power to help other blacks who were unjustly tried.

Kennedy called local officials and urged them to reconsider King's severe jail sentence. King was finally released. He immediately set about planning further action.

It was proposed that the sit-ins be "put on the road." Groups of blacks and whites together boarded interstate buses stopping from town to town testing their rights to use lunchrooms and waiting rooms labeled for whites only. They were called Freedom Riders.

Violence erupted. Several of the riders were severely beaten. A bus was set on fire. Instead of discouraging the Freedom Riders, it brought more people to their side for demonstrations.

King realized that what the civil rights movement needed now was an overall plan. He knew that not all

Hostile whites abused demonstrators who were trying to gain equal rights to use public facilities.

their goals could be reached at once, so it was decided to concentrate on one community at a time. Birmingham, Alabama, was perhaps the most thoroughly segregated large city in the South. In January 1963 Martin Luther King, Jr., announced that he would be going to Birmingham to fight the segregation laws still enforced by the city government.

It started with several small sit-ins where the demonstrators were arrested and sent off to jail. King and his helpers held nightly mass meetings trying to encourage others to join their nonviolent "army."

An injunction was issued by the Birmingham court forbidding any more demonstrations or public gatherings of any size. King felt that this was an unjust law and the only way to get a public hearing was to demonstrate by marching to city hall. The Commissioner of Public Safety, Eugene "Bull" Connor, was the one to enforce the law.

Fifty volunteers led by King and Rev. Ralph Abernathy, a close friend and tireless fighter for civil rights, started the march. They were arrested and taken off to jail. King was put in a cell by himself. He spent his time writing a long letter in answer to his critics, who protested that the demonstrations he had organized were "unwise and untimely."

That letter became an often quoted statement of his philosophy, a classic explanation of the civil rights movement. His critics had asked why he felt direct action was necessary when he was so opposed to violence. Why not negotiate?

"You are exactly right in your call for negotiation," he wrote. "Indeed this is the purpose of direct action. . . . It seeks so to dramatize the issue that it can no longer be ignored . . . to create a situation so crisis-packed that it will inevitably open the door to negotiations."

King defended his actions of urging his followers to break the law by marching through the streets and holding demonstrations. "Any law that degrades human personality is unjust. All segregation statutes are unjust because segregation distorts the soul and damages the personality."

His letter was published in newspapers all over the country. Eight days later King was released from jail, but others took up the challenge. Every day there were peaceful demonstrations. Even children joined the marchers. The police retaliated with water hoses, tear gas, and dogs. The news media recorded everything on film. For the first time people all over the world could see the brutality used against blacks. Some said that "Bull" Connor did more to help the civil rights movement than any other white in the South by displaying such cruelty and hatred. Many were ashamed and vowed to help change the discrimination.

The jails filled with blacks. Downtown stores were boycotted by blacks. Whites stayed away as well. Something had to be done.

After a meeting with Dr. King and other black leaders, an interracial committee was formed to ensure that segregation of public places would be eliminated and that black clerks and salespersons would be hired whenever there were openings. Progress was made, but violence did not end overnight. Instead, some of the bloodiest days were ahead.

# 6

# *Free at Last*

To continue the fight for progress and to celebrate the hundredth anniversary of the Emancipation Proclamation, black leaders planned a mass meeting in the nation's capital in 1963. People came from all over the country, families saving to make the trip any way they could, by bus, on foot, sharing rides. They came to show Congress that they wanted laws passed giving black people their civil rights.

On the appointed day, August 28, 1963, two hundred thousand people gathered in front of the Lincoln Memorial. Many sympathetic whites had made the trip too. It was a peaceful group, not a defiant mob as had been feared.

Prayers were said, hymns sung. There were many speakers, but it was the words of Martin Luther King, Jr., telling the audience of his dreams for the future that struck the conscience of the world.

"Nineteen sixty-three is not an end, but a beginning. . . . We must always march ahead. We cannot turn back. There are those who are asking the devotees of civil rights, 'When will you be satisfied?' We can never be satisfied as long as the Negro is the victim of the unspeakable horrors of police brutality. . . . We can never be satisfied as long as our bodies, heavy with fatigue of travel, cannot gain lodging in the motels of the highways and the hotels of the cities. We cannot be satisfied as long as the Negro's basic mobility is from a smaller ghetto to a larger one.

"We can never be satisfied as long as our children are stripped of their selfhood and robbed of their dignity by signs stating 'for whites only.' We cannot be satisfied as long as a Negro in Mississippi cannot vote and a Negro in New York believes he has nothing for which to vote.

"I have a dream my four little children will one day live in a nation where they will not be judged by the color of their skin but by the content of their character. . . . I have a dream that one day little black boys

President Kennedy receiving Martin Luther King, Jr., and other leaders of the August 28, 1963 march on Washington

and black girls will be able to join hands with little white boys and white girls as sisters and brothers. I have a dream today!"

It seemed such a simple dream, but within a month the country was shocked with the news of the bombing of a black church in Birmingham. Four little girls attending Sunday school were killed. It was a time of sorrow.

During this period of violence, the words and deeds of Martin Luther King, Jr., were singled out for international honor. Early in 1964 King was nominated for the Nobel Peace Prize given to the individual or organization who "had contributed the most to the furtherance of peace among men."

Here was proof that his message of peace to the world had been heard. He was fighting not only for peace between races of different color but for peace between warring countries.

Martin Luther King, Jr., receives the Nobel Peace Prize.

King accepted the award humbly "in the name of all men who love peace and brotherhood." He divided the $54,000 prize among various civil rights organizations.

Earlier in the year a Civil Rights Act was signed into law by President Lyndon Johnson. It guaranteed there would be no segregation in any public accommodations throughout the country. But again these rights had to be fought for—this time in Selma, Alabama.

During January and February of 1965, there were several marches and demonstrations in Selma that resulted in mass arrests. The protests were against the voting registration officials who did everything in their power to keep blacks from adding their names to the voting lists. In some towns a prospective voter was required to have two registered voters to vouch for him. Since no blacks were registered, and no whites would sign for a black, the would-be voters were turned away.

National interest in the campaign was light until on February 18 Jimmie Lee Jackson, a twenty-six-year-old black man, was fatally shot by state troopers during a demonstration. A number of other protesters were viciously beaten.

This was enough to enflame sentiment. King and the Southern Christian Leadership Conference proposed a march from Selma to the state capital in Montgomery, a distance of fifty-four miles, to demand reforms. Nearly six hundred marchers assembled, most with food, bedrolls, and blankets they'd need for the trip.

They met no resistance for the first six blocks, but as they turned to cross a highway bridge, their way was blocked by a wall of state troopers. Speaking through a bullhorn, the head of the police force gave the marchers a three-minute warning to turn back of their own accord or force would be used.

The first line of marchers knelt on the pavement. Others followed the same action. Within minutes the troopers advanced with clubs, whips, and tear gas.

"It was like a battle zone," remembers John Lewis, one of the leaders, whose own skull was fractured in the fighting.

The marchers were driven back to the church where they had started, while whites lined the sidewalk cheering. More than sixty demonstrators were treated for injuries at the church. Seventeen others had to be carried to the hospital.

Two young ministers, one black and one white, were beaten to death. One woman was shot. It was the most violent confrontation King had experienced. He grieved that peaceful negotiations had not prevented bloodshed. Newspaper headlines called it "Bloody Sunday," but King announced that he and Rev. Abernathy would lead another march on March 9, in spite of the fact that a United States Federal Court had issued a temporary injunction against such action.

King spoke to the crowds that backed him. "The only way we can really achieve freedom is to somehow conquer the fear of death. But if a man has not discovered something that he will die for, he isn't fit to live. . . . We've gone too far to turn back now. We must let them know that nothing can stop us—not even death itself. We must be ready for a season of suffering."

Over fifteen hundred marchers, some from other parts of the country, came to Selma to show their support. Again police blocked their way. Again the protesters were turned back with force.

That same day, a federal court finally overruled the city of Selma's ban on demonstrations. The way was legally cleared for the march to take place, although the judge had set up a compromise ruling that only three hundred marchers were to be allowed past the first eight miles of the route.

Nearly twenty-five thousand sympathizers arrived in Montgomery to greet the three hundred pilgrims who had walked the entire way. They were greeted by a chorus of "We Shall Overcome."

Through their determined effort, King and his followers did overcome the stumbling block to one of their major goals. On August 6, 1965, a voting rights bill was passed. No more literacy tests were required. Blacks had the right to vote.

In other parts of the country blacks were turning to violence. In Watts, a part of Los Angeles, a minor scuffle with police turned to rioting, burning, and looting. Radical civil rights leaders were calling for displays of black power.

"You'll never win with violence," King told them, but not all listened.

King realized that poverty caused much of the unrest. Blacks were often forced to live in crowded run-down tenements. Better jobs, better working conditions; this is where he planned to turn his efforts. Not only blacks, but poor whites, Hispanics, and Asians needed his help. He planned a poor people's march to Washington. "Bread, not bombs," he declared.

At the same time he was speaking out for world peace, United States troops were fighting in Vietnam.

He urged President Johnson to end the war. Johnson felt that he had helped blacks in their fight for civil rights and that King was being unfair by repaying him with harsh criticism. But Dr. King would not give up his campaign for world peace. He continued to write and speak out against the country's involvement in Vietnam. Finally world pressure convinced the president that troops should be brought home.

But there were still battles at home King had to fight. In 1966, Dr. King went to Chicago to lend his support to fight residential discrimination. Mayor Richard Daley greeted him with vague promises, but no real changes were made.

In 1968 he traveled to Memphis, Tennessee, to help the sanitation workers out on strike. He was a man who tried to be everywhere at once and still have time with his wife and children. He set himself an impossible schedule.

On April 3 he gave his last sermon. It was almost as if he knew what was going to happen to him.

"We've got some difficult days ahead. But it doesn't matter with me now. Because I've been to the mountaintop. And I don't mind. Like anybody, I would like to live a long life. Longevity has its place. But I'm not concerned about that now. I just want to do God's will. And He's allowed me to go up to the mountain. And I've looked over. And I've seen the promised land. I may not get there with you. But I want you to know tonight, that we, as a people will get to the promised land. And I'm happy, tonight. I'm not worried about anything. I'm not fearing any man. Mine eyes have seen the glory of the coming of the Lord."

He gave hope to his followers that changes for good were ahead for them. Martin Luther King, Jr., was not to see these further changes in his lifetime. The next day as he was leaving his motel room to go to dinner, a shot rang out. The bullet hit him in the neck. Within minutes he was dead.

The world had lost a great leader. King had fired the hopes of minority groups. He had shown them the way to achieve self-respect. He had done much to change the conscience of the world.

On his tombstone are carved the words "Free at Last!"

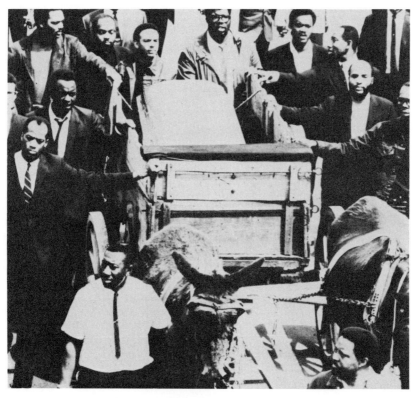

Martin Luther King, Jr.'s funeral procession

# 7

# *The Center*

The nation felt sorrow, shock, and grief. Martin Luther King, Jr., had been assassinated at thirty-nine, at the very height of his career. The first reaction of many blacks was to fight back. Black militants marched through city streets, arming themselves with weapons, raising clenched fists in the sign of black power.

King's death touched off the most widespread racial violence in the nation's history. There were riots in more than 130 cities. Before it was over thirty-nine people had died and countless others had been injured. King had opposed such tactics during his life, but after his death no black leader emerged to bring the mob under control.

Floyd McKissick, a member of the Congress of Racial Equality (CORE), declared, "Dr. Martin Luther King, Jr. was the last prince of nonviolence. Non-violence is a dead philosophy, and it was not the black people that killed it. It was the white people who killed nonviolence."

President Johnson appealed to the public to remember King's own words. "No one could doubt what Martin Luther King would want. That his death should be the cause of more violence would deny everything he worked for."

Dr. L. Harold De Wolfe, one of King's former teachers, told mourners, "It is for us to finish his work, to end the awful destruction in Vietnam, to root out every trace of prejudice from our lives, to bring the massive powers of this nation to the aid of the oppressed and to heal the hate-scarred world."

But how could his unfinished work be carried on? How could his unfulfilled dreams be realized? How could he best be honored?

There were many black leaders who had worked closely with King during his lifetime, but the person closest to him, his wife, Coretta Scott King, was the one who first stepped forward to organize the Martin Luther King, Jr., Center for Nonviolent Social Change to continue his unfinished business.

The tremendous scope of the plan discouraged some. Just the job of raising funds and designing the Center to accommodate the various functions Coretta envisioned seemed impossible. Raising money for the relief of the poor and disadvantaged should come first, some said. But Mrs. King would not give up.

She spoke to the many friends Martin Luther King, Jr., had left behind, trying to persuade them that the Center would draw people together for the very purpose of solving these problems. It would be a living symbol of King's philosophy of change through nonviolent action.

She feared that young blacks might not remember what life had been like before King's fight for social justice. They might become complacent and stop their struggle for further progress. There was still so much to be done: poverty and war still had to be overcome. Only through a central office could the work across the nation be organized.

Her enthusiasm won support for the idea. The first plans for the Center were drawn up in 1968. Rev. Leslie H. Carter explained that the original purpose was to provide meeting rooms for those working on programs which some day would eliminate the suffering caused by poverty, violence and racism.

The Freedom Hall Complex opened on January 15, 1982. It represented an investment of nearly $10 million, money that was donated by business, labor, and religious groups and in part by federal agencies and by foreign governments. The year after its opening, approximately four hundred thousand persons visited the facilities.

The King Center buildings are located on a forty-four-acre site designated as a National Historic District. It includes the home where Dr. King was born and the Ebenezer Baptist Church, where three generations of Dr. King's family preached.

The church is a small, simple structure. The walls are white. Stained glass windows in blues and green send rays of light across the plain wooden pews. Behind the pulpit, where Dr. King preached, is a white cross illuminated with lights. Martin Luther King, Jr.'s mother used to play the organ here. She was shot during a service in 1974.

Close by is the tomb where Martin Luther King, Jr., is buried, set in a brick circular pavilion surrounded by a reflecting pool that flows down several levels. On the tomb itself are carved the words, "Free at last, free at last; thank God Almighty, we are free at last."

The rest of the complex is a busy place. The Community Center houses an early learning center, a library, family and childrens' services offices, a combination gymnasium and auditorium, an Olympic-size swimming pool, and arts and crafts facilities. Outside there are other areas for sports. There are a museum, gift shop, bookstore, and cafeteria.

What goes on inside this complex is exciting. The Center helps set up programs for other minority groups. Over 15 million people of Hispanic heritage live in the United States, many facing problems similar to those blacks have had to deal with. The Center has researched ways to provide better housing for the underprivileged, by both restoring existing buildings and advising government and private enterprises in constructing new buildings.

Voter education and training to encourage more blacks to run for local and national offices in government is offered. The King Center helps train volunteer tutors who give remedial help to youths and adults who need schooling in basic math and reading to prepare for better jobs. Scholarships are awarded to gifted students.

Charlie Davis knows what King's Memorial Center is like. Charlie dropped out of school when he was ten, after his father was hurt in an accident. Charlie could only earn a little at odd jobs, but it helped buy the family food. Charlie never went back to school. He's nineteen now, but he'd never really learned how to read or write or figure very well. Even filling out papers to apply for a job was hard.

Someone told him about the remedial program at the Center where he wouldn't have to start over with little kids in the first grade. Charlie comes to the Center every evening to get help. He's working in a hardware store now, able to keep records and list inventory. Some day he hopes to be a manager or even an owner of a store.

These are just some of the things others have been inspired to do following in the footsteps of Martin Luther King, Jr.

Coretta Scott King speaks at a reception in honor of her husband. She has carried on his legacy.

# 8

# *Honoring Martin Luther King, Jr.*

Since Martin Luther King's death, many memorials have been built. Schools, hospitals, streets, bridges, and works of art have all been dedicated to his memory. His bust is displayed in the Georgia state capital, where once he would not have been welcome, and another is in the Capitol Rotunda in Washington, D.C.

In Memphis, where his life abruptly ended, there is a Dr. Martin Luther King, Jr., Expressway. Community centers, public housing developments, and social service centers throughout the country bear his name.

All over the world he has been remembered. His picture has been used on postage stamps. In Israel a forest of trees was planted in his memory. A church in Hungary is dedicated to King because of his work for world peace.

On the very first year the holiday was celebrated, cards were distributed by the King Center in Atlanta asking people to pledge, "I commit myself to living the dream of loving, not hating, showing understanding, not anger, making peace, not war."

Some communities decided to honor King on his holiday by selecting a theme, such as better housing for the poor, and parading peacefully through the streets to publicize that need. In schools, the story of the marches in Birmingham, Selma, and Little Rock were told and reenacted.

Most young people today are unaware of what life was like for blacks when Martin Luther King, Jr., started his civil rights campaign. Andy Sellmer's father knows. He was one of the first black students at a white school in his hometown in Virginia. He was yelled at and cursed that first morning he dared enter the front door. No one told him where he was supposed to go for classes. It was a lonely and frightening feeling, knowing that people

Dedication of a bust of Martin Luther King, Jr., in Harlem, New York April 4, 1970

hated him just because he was black.

Now that he is a grown man with a family, he has helped Andy make a list of some of the changes that have come about. Black students and white students now share the same lunchroom, use the same washrooms, and are allowed to be on athletic teams and take part in all school activities together.

No one has to sit at the back of buses or in the top balcony at a movie theater any more, and Andy's mom and dad have been able to vote for blacks running for public office.

Black TV and movie stars and other blacks have been specially honored in art, music, and science. Black astronauts, men and a woman, have been selected to explore the mysteries of outer space in the future.

But when Andy went to school the teacher made

Second graders from McGogney Elementary School in Washington, D.C., presenting a program in celebration of the Martin Luther King, Jr., holiday

them make a list of some of the goals Martin Luther King, Jr., had set that have not been met. On the bulletin board were pictures of dilapidated, run-down buildings where the poor were herded together in cramped living quarters, not much better than the slave quarters Andy's great-grandparents had had to share.

"Why didn't they move out?" someone asked. Andy knew. Jobs were hard to come by, and even with a good education Andy's dad didn't receive the same pay for the same work as a white person. There was still prejudice.

The teacher asked everyone to think of ways they could help stop prejudice. What would Martin Luther King, Jr., have told them?

King had said that everybody could help. Blacks and whites alike could reach out and get to know someone who is "different" in skin color, in heritage, or someone who might believe in a different religion. Even a handshake or a smile was a good start. And if there was someone who had made you angry, you should try to make up and become friends. Andy could do that.

On King's holiday the Sellmer family hung an American flag from their front porch. Church bells rang, and people were asked to turn on their car headlights at noon to remind everyone this was a special day. There was a picture on television of schoolchildren in Arizona letting hundreds of balloons sail up in the sky. There were organized marches in over three hundred cities across the country.

Many people went to church that day to hear the words of Martin Luther King, Jr., repeated. "True justice must be colorblind. Among black and white Americans, their destiny is tied up with our destiny, and their freedom is inextricably bound to our freedom; we cannot walk alone," he had said.

As part of the national celebration, the fifty states were asked by the King holiday commission to locate the replicas of the Liberty Bell sent to them by President Harry Truman during World War II and to ring them at exactly 12:00 noon on King's holiday. Truman sent the bells to remind Americans during the war years of the price paid for their liberty. The organizers of the bell ringing in King's honor hope that this act will encourage people to commit themselves to the fight for freedom and justice for everyone in the country regardless of race, creed or sex.

Today many people use King's memory in their crusade for the end of racism.

Coretta Scott King asked Americans to rededicate themselves to the commandments King believed in and tried to live every day of his life. "Thou shalt love thy God with all thy heart, and thou shalt love thy neighbor as thyself."

"It is no longer a question of violence or non-violence. It is nonviolence or nonexistence."

Communities planned together, blacks and whites, to make the holiday a not-to-be-forgotten day. Black leaders who had made contributions in the fields of social service, politics, cultural arts, education, sports, entertainment, or science were honored on King's day. Musical programs have been dedicated to his memory, combining old Negro spirituals with new compositions

King is honored by a boys' choir at the Schomburg Center in New York City.

from such artists as Stevie Wonder, who had worked hard to make the day a national holiday.

On his holiday people bow their heads in prayer for other oppressed people around the world, especially for blacks in South Africa, who have little chance of living a life of freedom, respect, or anything but the pain of poverty.

Martin Luther King, Jr.'s day is a time for memories. Some of the people who knew him best have shared their thoughts.

Julian Bond, a black congressman from Georgia, felt King's most important contribution was "that he made popular the idea that individuals are capable of changing their situation. Through the protests of the 1960's, it was demonstrated that people could do that."

Rev. Jesse Jackson remembers that "the so-called 'I have a dream' speech was not a speech about dreams and dreaming. It was a speech about nightmare conditions. Dr. King was not assassinated for dreaming." He was assassinated for bringing about change that some whites did not want, but he told the world, "The gap between your words and actions must close." Too many people said they sympathized with the civil rights movement but did little to help the cause.

The message King gave to Rev. Jackson was that "we must use what we've got, and God will give the increase." This means God would help those who helped themselves.

Jackson admitted that King "had an extraordinary mind, but he cultivated and developed it through disciplined study—and then applied it to the process of social change."

Dr. T. J. Jeminson, president of the National Baptist Convention U.S.A., Inc., said, "Dr. King left for all of us, not only black people, but for all Americans, the goal of making this nation and the world one: one in hope, one in aims, one in ideals."

Senator Edward Kennedy reminds us that King "dedicated his life to completing the unfinished business of the American Revolution and the Civil War."

U.S. Representative Mary Rose Oakar wrote that, "Jefferson gave us our Declaration of Independence, which says that all men are created equal, and Dr. King was the most significant modern American exponent of this ideal. . . . As a woman, I think his interest in equality was an impetus toward action on behalf of women. The elderly who experience age discrimination also can identify with his crusade."

Rev. Ralph David Abernathy, one of his closest friends, remembers King as "an eloquent speaker, as a brave warrior, as an intellectual who never lost the common touch, as a witty man with a delightful sense of humor, as a great leader who met with presidents and kings, as the brother who marched with sharecroppers and sanitation workers, as the catalyst for social change during a turbulent era."

Dr. King celebrated his own last birthday before his murder in the basement of the Ebenezer Baptist Church planning the Poor People's Campaign. Let's honor him by carrying on his work.

# Important Dates

January 15, 1929. Martin Luther King, Jr., is second of three children born to Rev. Martin Luther King, Sr., and Mrs. Alberta Christine Williams King in Atlanta, Georgia.

September 1944. King enters Morehouse College at fifteen.

February 15, 1948. King is ordained a Baptist minister.

September 1948. King enters Crozer Theological Seminary.

September 1951. King continues his studies at Boston University and meets his future wife.

June 18, 1953. King marries Coretta Scott at her home in Heiberger, Alabama.

September 1, 1954. King accepts the position of pastor of the Dexter Avenue Baptist Church in Montgomery, Alabama.

June 5, 1955. King is awarded a Ph.D. in systematic theology at Boston University.

December 1, 1955. Mrs. Rosa Parks is arrested for not giving up her seat to a white man on a public bus. King organizes Montgomery bus boycott.

January 10–11, 1957. The Southern Christian Leadership Conference is formed. Dr. King is elected its first president.

September 9, 1957. The first civil rights act since Reconstruction is passed by Congress, creating the Civil Rights Commission and the Civil Rights Division of the Department of Justice.

September 20, 1958. King is stabbed in Harlem.

February 2–March 10, 1959. Dr. and Mrs. King visit India studying Mahatma Gandhi's techniques of nonviolent protest.

January 24, 1960. The Kings move to Atlanta, where Dr. King becomes co-pastor with his father of the Ebenezer Baptist Church.

August 28, 1963. The largest integrated mass protest, a march on Washington, is held. King delivers his "I Have a Dream" speech before 250,000 people at the Lincoln Memorial.

December 10, 1964. Dr. King receives the Nobel Peace Prize in Oslo, Norway.

April 3, 1968. Dr. King delivers his "I've Been to the Mountaintop" speech in Memphis.

April 4, 1968. Martin Luther King, Jr., is shot and killed at the Lorraine Motel in Memphis.

# Further Reading

Adler, David A. *Martin Luther King, Jr.* New York: Holiday House, 1986.

Bains, Rae. *Martin Luther King.* Mahwah, N.J.: Troll Associates, 1985.

Davidson, Margaret. *I Have a Dream: The Story of Martin Luther King.* New York: Scholastic, 1986.

Faber, Doris, and Faber, Harold. *Martin Luther King, Jr.* New York: Julian Messner, 1986.

Jones, Margaret. *Martin Luther King, Jr.* Chicago: Children's Press, 1968.

McKissack, Patricia. *Martin Luther King, Jr.: A Man to Remember.* Chicago: Childrens Press, 1984.

Millender, Dharathula H. *Martin Luther King, Jr.: Young Man With a Dream.* New York: Macmillan Publishing Co., 1986.

Milton, Joyce. *Marching to Freedom: The Story of Martin Luther King, Jr.* New York: Dell Publishing Co., 1987.

Peck, Ira. *The Life and Words of Martin Luther King, Jr.* New York: Scholastic, 1986.

Schulke, Flip, and McPhee, Penelope O. *King Remembered.* New York: W. W. Norton & Co., 1986.

Webb, Sheyann, and Nelson, Rachel W. *Selma, Lord, Selma: Girlhood Memories of the Civil-Rights Days.* Tuscaloosa: University of Alabama Press, 1980.

# Index